The Rainy Picnic

GAZELLE BOOKS

Fire-Brigade Willie
Special Branch Willie
Upsidedown Willie
DOROTHY CLEWES

The Little Sparrow
The Donkey Upstairs
FRANCES EAGAR

The Rocking Horse
ROSEMARY MANNING

The Picnic Dog
Worm Weather
CHRISTOBEL MATTINGLEY

Fish and Chips
The Big Show
The Tractor
Sports Day
PAMELA ROGERS

Michael and the Dogs
ELFRIDA VIPONT

and many other titles

PAMELA ROGERS

The Rainy Picnic

Illustrated by
PRISCILLA CLIVE

HAMISH HAMILTON
London

First published in Great Britain 1972
by Hamish Hamilton Children's Books Ltd
90 Great Russell Street, London WC1B 3PT

SBN 241 02147 2

Printed by photolithography and bound in
Great Britain at The Pitman Press, Bath

It was raining. Out in the kitchen, all neatly packed in the wicker basket, was a picnic.

"Oh bother, bother!" said Michael.

Michael's mother came and stood by the window too. She peered out.

"Oh dear," she said. "It *does* look black, doesn't it?"

"You *said* we should have a picnic today," said Michael. "You promised!"

His mother sighed.

"Now, Michael, don't let's go through all that again! I didn't make it rain," she said. "Besides, even if it had been fine, I don't know about baby. She doesn't seem well."

At that moment, Michael's baby sister Sarah began to cry.

"Oh dear, there she goes again," said Michael's mother. "I'm ever so sorry, darling, but I'm afraid a picnic is out of the question."

Then she hurried off out of the room to see to the baby.

Michael scowled at his own reflection in the window-pane. He had been looking forward to this picnic for a long time. Early that morning, the sky had been all red and fine. The sun had been shining. He had really thought it was going to be a lovely day.

The front gate clicked. Michael looked out. Someone was coming up

the path. She had a thick black coat
and a squashy black hat. She stumped
through the puddles in rubber boots,
waving her large black umbrella.
"Ping" went the front-door bell. It
was Aunt Em. Aunt Em wasn't a

proper Aunt. She had known his mother when *she* was a little girl. Even now, she still told his mother what to do.

Michael heard the front door open.

"Land's sake, child," Michael heard Aunt Em say in her deep voice. "Don't keep me dripping on the step."

Michael could hear his mother explaining all about the baby, and the rain and the picnic that wasn't going to happen. He hoped she wouldn't invite Aunt Em into the front room. It wasn't that he was afraid of her exactly, he found her just a little alarming—especially when she looked at him hard through her glasses.

But Aunt Em came into the room, scattering raindrops off her boots and her large, beaky nose.

"What's this, then?" she said to Michael, prodding him with a long finger. "No picnic?"

Michael shook his head.

"Pshaw!" said Aunt Em. She turned to Michael's mother. "What about a wet picnic?" she said.

"A what?" said Michael and his mother together.

"A wet picnic, of course. Haven't you ever had one?"

Michael shook his head.

"Outside?" he said. "In the rain?"

"Oh, we couldn't," said his mother. "Really, Aunt Em. Just look at it! And if we could, Sarah isn't herself today. I wouldn't like to take her out in this."

"Who's suggesting you do?" said Aunt Em. "Young Michael and I will go. It's a long time, since I had a picnic—especially a wet one!"

Michael's mother was still doubtful.

"I don't know," she said. "Really, I don't." She looked at Michael.

But Michael was looking at Aunt Em. She might look old—but she looked as if she *really* did want a picnic, just like him.

"Oh please, please," said Michael. "Let me go."

"Well, if you're sure," said his mother. "It's ever so nice of you, Aunt Em. Where will you go?"

Aunt Em pursed her lips.

"Ah," she said. "That's telling. Now Michael. Boots. Mac. Then we'll be off."

Aunt Em stumped upstairs to look at Sarah, while Michael's mother helped him to get ready. She gave him the picnic basket.

"You be a good boy," she said. "Do as you're told."

"I wish you and Sarah could come too," said Michael. "I really do."

"Oh, so do I," said his mother. "Another time."

Aunt Em came back.

"Teeth," she said. "That child's got teeth."

"What, Sarah?" said Michael's mother. "She hasn't got any yet?"

"She'll have one soon, mark my words. That's why she's fretty. You see."

Michael wished they would stop fussing over the baby and get on with the picnic.

But soon they were ready. Out in the rain they went under the big umbrella. Aunt Em walked quite quickly. She didn't go towards the park, where they always had their picnics. She went in the other direction.

"Where are we going?" said Michael.

"Bus stop," said Aunt Em briefly.

Very few people were there. One of the red buses drew up.

"Not ours," said Aunt Em, staring down the road. "Ah." She snapped her umbrella shut, showering rain down the neck of the man in front. "Whoops," she said, under her breath. Then she was waving wildly at the small green bus coming towards them.

"Stop!" she cried.

"This *is* a bus stop, lady," said the conductor, as they clambered on. "There's no need to shout."

"Pshaw!" said Aunt Em, waving a finger at him. "I like to make certain."

The conductor grinned.

"Where to, then?" he said.

"Pratt's End Farm," said Aunt Em, with satisfaction. "One and a half to Pratt's End Farm."

"It's as far as we go," said the conductor, punching out two white tickets.

"We're going to have a picnic," said Michael.

"Eh?" said the conductor. "In this rain?"

"Young man," said Aunt Em. "If you have never had a picnic in the rain, you've missed something."

The conductor pushed back his hat and scratched his head.

"You may be right," he said.

The country seemed very fresh and green in the rain.

"I wish Mummy could see this," said Michael.

"I expect she will," said Aunt Em. "Another time."

Michael frowned and shook his head.

"It's too far for baby," he said.

"Well, she won't be a baby for

ever," said Aunt Em.

Michael went on staring out.

"She does fuss so," he said.

Aunt Em gave a snort of laughter.

"Who?" she said. "Your mum or your sister?"

Michael looked round and began to smile.

"Both," he said.

"Bound to," said Aunt Em. "It was just the same with you, when you were young and helpless."

"I suppose it was," said Michael.

"Young things. . . ," said Aunt Em. "They grow up very soon."

"Hey," said the conductor, coming down the bus towards them. "There's a sight for sore eyes, and no mistake."

Michael and Aunt Em looked out. They were right at the top of the hill.

It was still raining around them, but on the horizon the sky was bright. Grey scarves of cloud drifted along the green fields. They could see the silver glint of a river.

Aunt Em nodded with satisfaction.

"Gosh!" said Michael.

"You know these parts?" said the

conductor to Aunt Em.

"Know them?" said Aunt Em. "Like the back of my hand."

"I thought so," said the conductor. "We're nearly there."

The rain was still coming down. Michael began to wonder where they would eat their picnic. The bus stopped.

Aunt Em got up. Her umbrella caught in one of the seats. "Whoops-a-daisy," she said, annoyed, tugging it. "Come here, you stupid thing."

"Leave us a bit of bus," said the conductor, but he was laughing. "Have a good time."

"Come on, young Michael," said Aunt Em. "Best boot forward."

The bus turned round and went back the way it had come. Michael waved to the cheeky conductor. Aunt Em was sniffing the air like a war-horse.

"If you can't keep yourself under the umbrella," she said, "keep the

food under it. Most important. Follow me."

Michael followed. Their boots squelched in the mud. They reached a stile. Aunt Em glared at it.

"Stupid things," she said. "Why can't they have a good, sensible gate. Oh well, here goes."

"Can you manage?" said Michael doubtfully.

"Manage—ooh," said Aunt Em crossly. "Of course—whoops!—I can manage."

With grunts and umbrella waving wildly, Aunt Em climbed the stile.

"Child's—puff, puff—play," she
said.

Michael noticed there were cows in
the field.

"Er . . . do you mind cows, Aunt
Em?" he asked.

Michael *did* rather mind cows. He
thought they were rather large alarming

creatures.

Aunt Em looked sideways at Michael through her glasses.

"You *might* say 'do cows mind me'?" she said. "When I get really wild with a cow, it's the *cow* that runs." She brandished her umbrella and the nearest cow gave a startled moo and lolloped away.

After that, Michael felt Aunt Em could manage anything. He followed her across the field and there was the farm house.

"Pratt's End Farm," said Aunt Em, before he could ask. "Onward, young Michael!"

Twirling her umbrella, she strode briskly into the farmyard by the muddy path. There were some very deep puddles.

Michael could hear some very deep mutters coming from Aunt Em, as her boots sank into them.

Out of a nearby building came a large, burly figure. He had a piece of sacking spread over his shoulders to keep out the wet and a soft, squashy cap.

"Terrible state this path, Fred," said Aunt Em to him, for all the world as if she had been having a conversation for hours.

"Em! By all that's wonderful!" A great smile spread over the man's face.

He strode over to her and seized both her hands, umbrella and all, and began to shake them.

"What brings you here?" he asked.

"Why not?" said Aunt Em. "We're having a wet picnic. Meet young Michael. Michael—meet an old friend of mine."

Fred seized Michael's hand in his great one and pumped it up and down.

"Hello," said Michael.

"Have it in the barn—your picnic—" cried Fred. "Just the place for it. Come on!"

"We-e-ll," said Aunt Em, pursing her lips doubtfully. "We-e-ll. I'm not sure . . ."

"Come and see," said Fred.

Michael looked at Aunt Em. She gave him a quick sideways look and nodded. A gleam shone in her eyes. Michael knew she had *meant* to have the picnic in the barn, all the time.

"All right," said Aunt Em to Fred. "If you *insist*!"

They went into the barn. The wide doors were open. It was the nicest possible sort of place. One side of it was full to the brim with sweet-smelling hay bales. The floor was covered with a soft scattering of it. Up in the rafters, a couple of doves cooed and billed. From the doors, they could see the hills.

"Wait," said Fred. "I'll get a blanket."

Aunt Em was looking out at the rain-swept scene.

"Quite like old times," she said.

Fred came back with an old brown blanket. He spread it neatly with his big, gnarled hands and stepped back.

"All yours, Em and young Michael," he said.

Aunt Em nodded. She flicked a corner of the blanket straight with her umbrella, prodded here and there, and nodded again.

"That'll do nicely, thank you, Fred,"
she said. "Quite-oo-er-comfortable,"
she added, as she lowered herself
down.

Michael put the basket in between
them and sat down too.

"You got work, Fred?" said Aunt
Em. "Don't mind us. Off you go.
We're fine."

It was warm and rustly in the barn.

Outside the rain stopped coming down in long straight rods. It began to patter and almost stop. A delicious smell of wet grass came blowing in.

"Ah," said Aunt Em. "That gives me an appetite. Open that basket, Michael."

Michael opened the packets. There were egg sandwiches and cheese and tomato sandwiches. There was lettuce and crispy celery to crunch. There were chocolate biscuits and crisps. There was a bottle of milk, and a

bottle of orange.

"My word," said Aunt Em. "I'll say this for your mum—she knows how to make a good picnic. Let's tuck in."

"It's specially nice here," said Michael. "I thought we would have wet sandwiches outside."

"Did you now?" said Aunt Em. "I'm surprised you came then. I don't like wet sandwiches either." She chuckled. "But I expect your poor Mum's seeing us, crouched under a tree, catching the drips off our hats!"

Fred came back with an armful of kittens. He dropped them in Michael's lap—black and white, tabby and one very small ginger one.

"Thought you'd like to see them,"

he said.

Michael picked them up. Their tiny little bodies were warm and wriggly. They dug into his trousers with needle-sharp claws.

"Where's the mother?" said Michael.

"Having a rest," said Fred. "Mind you, when they were young and help-less she'd fuss over them for hours— but they're growing up now."

"Told you," said Aunt Em. "They all grow up."

One kitten leapt across and landed on her shoulder. It mewed.

"He-o-lp. He-o-lp," it said.

Another one followed.

"Well," said Aunt Em. "I've heard of fur-fashions, but *this* is ridiculous. Here, Michael." She plucked them off.

They scampered away, except the small ginger one. He curled up against Michael and went to sleep.

By the time the last crumb was eaten, the rain had stopped. An occasional drip from the eaves of the barn reminded them of the downpour. The puddles reflected back blue sky again.

"Well," said Aunt Em. "Soon, we must make tracks homeward. It's quite a way. Don't want your mum thinking we've drowned."

"Just time to show the young'un the farm?" asked Fred, coming in.

"Just about," said Aunt Em. "I'll sit here and keep an eye on things."

Michael looked round. He couldn't see anything to keep an eye on.

"What things?" he said.

Fred nudged him and gave him a look.

"Of course!" he said to Aunt Em. "You do that, Em."

Michael tucked the kitten against his jacket. Before he and Fred had gone far, they could hear gentle snores coming from Aunt Em.

Michael and Fred grinned at each other.

"Women," said Fred.

Michael nodded. "I know," he said.

There were some lovely things to see on the farm—chickens, pigs, cows and a great black bull.

"Proper devil he can be," said Fred, leaning on the stout wooden gate of his pen. "But a good bull."

Michael was very glad that Aunt Em and the bull had not come face to face. He wasn't at all sure who would have come out best.

"Time to wake up, Em," said Fred, when they returned to the barn.

"Oo-er," said Aunt Em, waking up with a start. "Wake UP! I wasn't asleep, I was just shutting my eyes."

She struggled up.

"Don't - puff - help - phew - me. I'll manage," she said. "Now young Michael. Look sharp. Pick up our papers. All clean and tidy. I'm just going to have a word with Fred here."

Michael packed all the picnic remains away. He looked round to say goodbye to the ginger kitten, but it had gone.

Outside in the yard, Fred was starting the Land Rover.

"Nip in," he said to Michael. "I'm running you and Em to the bus stop. Save that walk across the fields."

With a rattling roar, they bumped up the track. The bus was waiting. It was the same conductor, leaning out. Aunt Em waved her brolly.

"Whoops," she said, as the conductor and Fred, one on each side, helped her aboard.

Her umbrella caught Fred's cap and pushed it over his eyes.

"Steady, Em," he said in his good-tempered way. "Come again soon—and young Michael."

"Sure to," said Aunt Em. "And thanks, Fred. It's been very nice."

"Oh, yes," said Michael. "It's been a lovely picnic."

They waved to Fred, until he was out of sight. The bus jolted on its way. Michael felt very sleepy. He noticed a basket, with a lid, on Aunt Em's lap.

"What's that?" he said.

"Eggs—and things," said Aunt Em.

Michael nodded. His eyes drooped and closed—rattle, rattle, squeak, roar went the wheels . . .

Michael woke up with a start.

"Quick march," said Aunt Em. "We're home."

Still half-asleep Michael got off. Down the road he could see his mother waiting for them, with Sarah in her arms.

"Oh," she cried, when they reached her. "You're not wet at all! Did you have a good time?"

"Pshaw!" said Aunt Em. "Of course we did."

"Show Aunt Em your tooth, then," said Michael's mother.

Michael saw a minute white speck of tooth on Sarah's gum. Aunt Em looked pleased.

"What did I say," she said. "Who's a clever girl."

"What a fuss," thought Michael, grinning to himself as he went inside with the picnic basket.

He could hear Aunt Em talking to his mother. Then—"Whoops!" she said. "My bus is due. I must hurry."

Before he could go out to thank her, she was off down the path.

Michael's mother put down Sarah and handed him the basket.

"Aunt Em left this," she said.

Michael took it. "It's eggs—and things," he said.

"He-o-lp," came the cry, from inside.

Michael flung back the lid. There *were* some eggs in egg boxes. Also, curled on a soft piece of flannel, was the ginger kitten.

"Oh," cried Michael. "Oh, Mummy! Is it for me to look after?"

His mother nodded. "That's what she said."

The noise of the bus came to them. Michael picked up the kitten and his mother picked up Sarah. Together they ran to the window.

Aunt Em was waving wildly at the bus to stop it. Michael saw her turn her sharp eyes and beaky nose towards the house.

He held the kitten up and waved its helpless little paw, and his mother held up Sarah to flap a pudgy pink hand.

Aunt Em lifted her brolly in a brief greeting. The handle caught slightly in the bus platform.

Michael saw her mouth move, though he could not hear.

"Whoops-a-daisy," she said. Then she got in the bus and was gone.